VEGETABLE SOUP

Featuring Jim Henson's Sesame Street Muppets

by Judy Freudberg and Tony Geiss

Illustrated by Tom Cooke

A SESAME STREET/GOLDEN PRESS BOOK
Published by Western Publishing Company, Inc.
in conjunction with Children's Television Workshop.

Library of Congress Catalog Card Number: 80-50849
ISBN 0-307-23114-3

"Oh-me-oh-my, me so hungry!" said Cookie Monster. He had been to the supermarket and was waiting for his groceries to be delivered.

"All me think about is cookies — beautiful Big Newtons! Oh! Where groceries? Where *COOKIES*??"

Then the doorbell rang.

"Me *eat*!" cried Cookie Monster, running to the door.

A delivery girl handed him a box of groceries.

Cookie Monster looked into the box. "Hey! These not Big Newtons. These not even cookies. What we have here?"

Cookie Monster tried to figure out what the things in the grocery box were.

"Long skinny orange thing look like pencil," he said, looking at a carrot. "Me sharpen it and write word 'cookie.'"

So he sharpened the carrot in a pencil sharpener and tried to write "cookie," but it didn't make a mark.

"Hmm. Maybe not pencil.
Maybe telescope!"

So he put the carrot to his
eye, but he couldn't see a thing.

"Wait! Me know!" he said,
picking up the whole bunch of
carrots. "Long orange things all
go together, and they are ... hat!"
And he put them on his head.

Then Cookie Monster took out the celery and tried to use it as a back scratcher, but it didn't work.

"Hmmm," he said. "This must be a bunch of pretty flowers!"

And he put it in a vase.

Next he tried to use the broccoli as a feather duster, but that didn't work, either. So he put it in the vase with the celery.

He picked up a beet and started it spinning like a top.

"Round and round and round it go," said Cookie Monster. "Where it stop, nobody know!"

Then he found a squash and put it to his ear.

"This must be telephone. Hello, operator?" he said, speaking clearly into the squash. But there was no reply.

Cookie Monster held up an onion.

"Small, white, round thing must be ball for playing jacks." So he tried to play jacks with the onion, but it wouldn't bounce.

Then he took out some potatoes. "Hmm, these funny looking things! Cowabunga!" he yelled and began to juggle the potatoes.

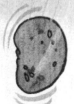

And just as he got them all in the air, Ernie and Bert came in with some bags of groceries.

"Me smell cookies!" yelled Cookie Monster, forgetting to juggle the potatoes. "Where you get cookies?"

"The supermarket made a mistake and sent your cookies to us and our groceries to you," said Bert.

"These things groceries?" cried Cookie Monster. "Hat, flowers, top, telephone, balls for jacks, things for juggling?"

"They're *vegetables*," said Ernie, as he and Bert began to gather them all up.

"This isn't a hat," said Bert, taking the carrots off Cookie Monster's head. "These are carrots."

"Hey, Ernie, why you take flowers out of vase?" asked Cookie Monster.

"These aren't flowers," said Ernie. "This is celery, and that is broccoli."

"And this is a beet, not a top," said Bert, as he stopped the spinning beet.

"You need to call somebody?" Cookie Monster asked when Ernie picked up the squash. "Don't bother. That telephone out of order."

"This isn't a telephone," said Ernie with a sigh. "It's a squash."

"Well, squash out of order."

Then Bert found the onion. "Hey, that my jacks ball!" Cookie Monster exclaimed.

"Don't be silly," said Bert. "It's an onion."

"And you were juggling potatoes!" said
Ernie. "You do funny things with
vegetables."

"What me supposed to do with them?" asked
Cookie Monster.

"Make vegetable soup, of course," said Bert.

"Oh ... what that?"

"Gosh, Cookie Monster," said Ernie. "You've
never heard of vegetable soup? It's delicious!"

"Vegetable soup as delicious as cookies?" asked Cookie Monster.

"More delicious than cookies," said Bert. "And almost as good as instant oatmeal."

"More delicious than cookies!" cried Cookie Monster. "Quick! Show me how to make vegetable soup! Please!"

So Ernie and Bert took the vegetables into the kitchen.

First Bert washed all the vegetables.
"Is it soup yet?" Cookie Monster asked.
"Oh no, Cookie Monster," replied Bert.
"We have to cook all the vegetables first."

So Bert put a pot of water on to boil. Then he cut up the carrots and potatoes and Ernie dropped them into the pot.

Then Bert chopped up the celery and Ernie dropped it into the pot.

"Is it soup yet?" asked Cookie Monster.

"Not yet," said Bert, as he cut up the broccoli.

Ernie dropped the broccoli into the pot.

Then Bert sliced the beet and the squash and Ernie dropped them into the pot.

"Mmm, vegetable soup smell good," said Cookie Monster.

"This is really hard work," said Ernie as
Bert peeled and cut up the onion. "Hurry up,
Bert. I'm hungry."

Then Ernie put the onion in the pot, and
Bert added salt and pepper.

And then they all waited and
sniffed and watched and got
hungrier and hungrier while the
vegetable soup cooked.

Finally, when the soup smelled just right, Bert turned off the stove.

"Is it soup yet?" asked Cookie Monster.

"Yes," said Bert. "The vegetable soup is cooked."

"Now we *eat*?" asked Cookie Monster.

"Not yet," said Ernie, putting the pot of soup on the table. "It's too hot to eat. You have to let it cool."

"But me so hungry!" moaned Cookie
Monster. "Me can't wait much longer!"
He stared at the steaming pot of soup.
"Me know!" said Cookie Monster, snapping
his fingers. "Me help cool soup."
So he started blowing on the soup.

Pretty soon Cookie Monster was out of breath, so he started fanning the soup with a newspaper.

"There must be easier way to cool soup," he said. "Aha! There is!"

And just as he aimed an electric fan at the soup, Bert shouted, "Wait, Cookie Monster! Don't do that. It's cool enough to eat now."

"SOOOUP!" yelled Cookie Monster, and he picked up the pot, opened his mouth, and swallowed all the vegetable soup in one big gulp.

"Mmm. Curiously refreshing," he said, wiping his mouth.

"Ulp," said Ernie.

"So that what to do with vegetables. Very interesting," said Cookie Monster. "Now me show you what to do with cookies.

"COOOOKIE!"

And he picked up the grocery bags and swallowed all the cookies.

"Cookies delicious!" sighed Cookie Monster.
"And you right, Ernie and Bert. Vegetable soup
delicious. Now, what for lunch?"

ABCDEFGHIJK